The Thoughts of a Small Orange Cat
by Anthony Ciccarelli

The old year has departed;
Now we have a new year to get started.
This girl has been at the party event,
But now she has new adventures to invent!

2

February arrives on the scene fast
With some guy who thinks he can forecast.
Out of the ground he pops, looking for shadows,
But I'm not sure if weather he knows!

As February gets to its center,
The noise builds of things running to enter.
Such a big sound stirs and pounds;
Soon it's everywhere - all around!

THUMP!
THUMP!
THUMP!
THUMP!
THUMP!
THUMP!
THUMP!
THUMP!
THUMP!
THUMP!
THUMP!
THUMP!

Here it comes!

4

There's clover all over! March is here,
And there are shamrocks everywhere!
Singing and dancing to be seen;
We look for luck in a sea of green!

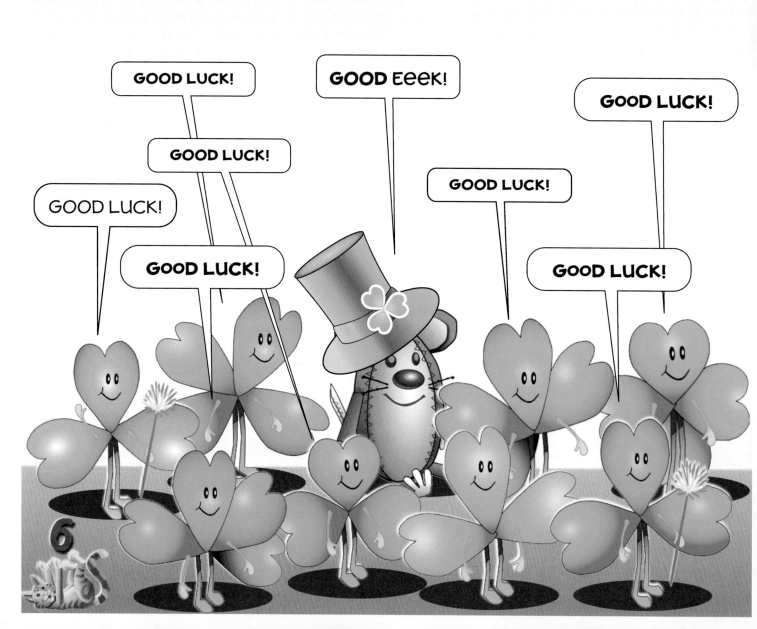

Months change all the while
With the eggs getting fancy new styles.
They sport colors that are very bright
With each one trying to look just right!

The eggs can't resist the urge to prance,
As around the counter they pose and dance.
I wait as they leave their basket to stroll
So I can make my move for control!

The eggs all gripe and whine,
But having a real "TREAT" in the basket is fine!
No matter how much they beg,
I remind them that "Cat always outranks Egg!"

A BOX! A BOX! What a magical place!
I can't wait to get in and play in this space!
That box can be whatever I want to see.
It can be a castle or fly to another galaxy!

You can't see me,
I'm in a box!

How can these walls of cardboard be so fun?
I don't know if I'll ever get done!
This box will travel to any place I crave,
Maybe an island, another planet or a giant cave!

13

Sometimes I imagine that I'm a piece of ancient stone
Hiding on a long lost island as my home.
I have wisdom of the past yet to be found
Waiting to change world history all around!

14

15

I dream I'm in a great cavern for my pleasure
On top of a huge hoard of treasure.
At a big, steamy dragon I do scoff.
My lunch was fish-flavored and my breath will run him off!

YIKES!

18

Change is in the air with the leaves,
But things are out of whack I believe.
There is something very strange about,
And what it is I have to find out!

To catch pests of corn candy design,
Being a corn candy cat works just fine!
The answer became easy for my mind to see.
No sweetie mice are going to "out-sweet" me!

THE
MONA GATTA

THE
MONA MOUSIE

At times I'd like to be art on the wall,
Displayed to be enjoyed by all.
Sitting in a museum in a shiny frame,
I am a portrait of great acclaim!

Museum Guide Book

You See 'um in the Museum!

Then again I'd like to be a cartoon,
Like on those shows watched in the afternoon.
I'd be animated and drawn using lines
In a clear and basic redesign!

I'm thinking all the time and that's the way to be.
Set your creativity free and you'll see.
Let you imagination roam about
And you'll be amazed by what comes out!

Dedications

To My Mom and Dad
Your endless support and
encouragement is unequaled.
Love you and thanks to you always!

To My Aunt Mary Ann

Auntie M, I treasure all the projects we've worked on together and look
forward to doing many more! All those fun things we kept putting together
gave me so many neat things to apply to this book. Love and thanks for
being one of my best supporters and most enthusiastic cheerleaders!

To Katherine Joyce

There are a few instructors in life whose teachings stay with us all of our
days due to their exemplary teaching skills. Katherine Joyce is one of
those instructors for me; as she was one of my high school English
teachers. I was honored for her to review this project as it neared its end.
So Mrs. Joyce, thanks so much for tolerating proofs and generating your
input to help tweak the text and grammatical choices; I just hope that I've
implemented everything properly. ;^)

To Small Orange Cats
Wow, no one will ever say you're sitting
there just napping again!

I thought I was
supposed to play
with the toys...

SMALL
ORANGE
SLIDE!

Yea!
Eeek!

BOiNG!

Advertisement!

If you like books about pets using their imagination...

Check out **"Super Sammie Saves the Day!"**, a book I wrote with Jeremy Uhrich and I
illustrated, using traditional illustration techniques with some work done with the
computer. I then assembled the parts of the book. The concept of exploring a pet's
imagination started out long ago in previous projects, and it continues on with **Sammie**.
Also, it's a **really** fun book!

dedications

Notes

• Hey, this is another title about "cat-magination" or "pet-magination"; and this silly, little picture book is done in a mixed media style, using collages of modified photographs and original artwork done with the computer. I've used this style many times over the last decade to create custom designs for greeting cards and wrapper boxes.

Many times when I'd go to the store to look for a greeting card; I'd like the image but not the sentiment inside or vice versa. So I worked to combine photographs (digital photographs or scans) and artwork to work together to create a card quickly. Need a Groundhog's Day card? It's no problem with this approach. Also you can make one card or a dozen quickly and easily using the computer and the printer. Much of the artwork done with the computer started out as hand sketches. Many of the scenes in the book are taken from these greeting cards or wrapper boxes.

It was a neat way to tie together many of these designs by using the **small orange cat** applying her imagination through the year as the focal point. The various characters presented within were very enjoyable to develop, so you may see them in some future books!

It is great to be able to take the mixed media of traditional art, computer art and photographic-based art and put them all together to tell a story. This approach can lead to endless options and opportunities that are fun to explore.

• No small orange cats (or any animals!) were harmed in the preparation of this book, but small orange cats may have been slightly annoyed by having numerous photographs taken (all without using a flash!).

• There are many wonderful cats and dogs looking for homes right now at your local shelter! Be sure to support your local shelter because they are doing a great thing, and they need our help. Also remember when you adopt a pet, you always need to put in the time and effort to create and maintain a lifelong bond yielding in **unconditional love**!

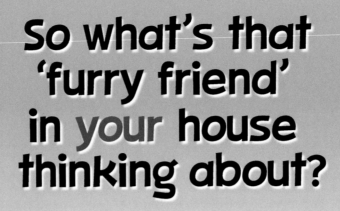

12/2019

Mac,
Let your imagination
roam free everyday —
it's a good thing to
do!

Anthony

Made in the USA
Columbia, SC
17 November 2018